MW01033951

THE KEYS TO THE KINGDOM

Elliott Downing

For Tracey

Ж

Press play.

Lines of store shelves viewed in grainy surveillance video. Cat food boxes, tubes of Pringles, the profile of a bearded clerk hunched over a book behind a counter. The security camera is mounted at the back of a convenience store, facing out over the rows of merchandise toward the shop's front door and floor-to-ceiling window. Some quirk of autofocus and relative light levels makes the world outside the shop clearer and better defined, on the screen, than the interior that the camera was theoretically installed to protect: sunlight shining on the street beyond the window; a single long, low car already halfway into view in the opening frame of the video, flitting briefly across the image from left to right and gone. A guitarist sits on the sidewalk across the street, his back to the wall beneath the window of a candle shop, his guitar case lying open on the concrete beside him to collect donations. A handful of other people pass up and down the sidewalks on either side of the street. What this camera must capture all day, every day: years upon years of never-viewed, never-remarked-upon footage. This 26-second snippet the rare, internet-worthy exception.

Angela enters from the left of the frame at the three-second mark, on the far side of the street, her head inclining slightly to watch the guitarist play as she steps around him. She's one more sidewalk figure among many; viewing her from this remove in grainy black and white, I wouldn't know it was her if I didn't know. I've tried watching the video in fullscreen to see her better, to try to learn if she was smiling or frowning or making any expression at all that afternoon, but I found that blowing up the low-res footage simply made her cloudy: a shadowy blob of pulsating, randomly-shifting gray boxes, barely recognizable as human at all. The video can only be understood, it seems, at smaller scales, as if viewed from a greater distance. Once I watched it while standing halfway across the room from the screen of my laptop and was startled by its apparent clarity.

I've memorized the five steps Angela takes after she passes the guitarist, a progression that both begins and ends with her right leg extended before her. Those steps have carried her well past the recessed doorway of the candle shop, a full three yards beyond the kill zone, before she stops and looks over her shoulder, lingering to hear more of the guitarist's music. Then she swings her extended foot around and takes four slower steps back the way she came, fishing into the purse at her side as she goes.

It's at this point that the white oval outline becomes superimposed around her body in the video, floating with her to track her progress back up the sidewalk, focusing the viewer's attention upon her: that implacable, non-negotiable halo with which YouTube marks its doomed.

There's no sound in the video. The moment of the gunshot can be discerned only in the reactions of the people on the screen: the guitarist's hands going suddenly still on their strings, the shop clerk's head lifting from his book, the half-dozen pedestrians on either side of the street all flinching and ducking and whipping their heads around at the same moment to locate the source of the noise. All of them but Angela who never heard it, Angela who, just now beginning her sideways topple into the candle shop's doorway, is already dead.

Some street dispute. Some random, stupid altercation. Far to the right of the frame, outside the view of this or any known camera, someone took a shot at someone else and missed – then, a fraction of a second later and twenty yards up the street, succeeded in making a different shot that even a master marksman would have struggled to replicate with a cheap pistol at that distance. In the video, Angela's body curls downward and strikes the sidewalk. She seems almost to stick to it, no smallest part of her rebounding from the concrete, just settling into this specific place as if it had been appointed to receive her. The white oval surrounding her body on the screen fades away now, its guidance no longer needed. The seated guitarist turns his head in Angela's direction, then lunges up onto his knees and scrambles toward her, his guitar rattling across the sidewalk behind him unnoticed, sliding to a halt with its neck extending over the edge of the curb. He reaches out as if to cup his hand beneath her head, then hesitates, seeing what's become of it. On the near side of the street, a long, low car drives partially into the frame from left to right, and the video ends.

Press replay. This time, the video is preceded by an ad for dog food. It runs for me several times a day now, always this same ad for this same brand, before Angela's final moments can play out again. There is nothing in the world any longer, it seems, that cannot be sponsored.

Ad completed; video resumes. The low-slung car flickers once again from left to right. The guitarist strums. Angela walks into view. Watching her, I find myself pleading for the smallest favors: willing the seated guitarist simply to be a slightly worse musician, a fraction less deserving of her attention, just for these next few seconds. Long enough for her to take another step or two down the sidewalk without pausing, for her to be allowed to flinch at the sound of the gunshot along with all the others, to look back and see the candle shop's front window shattering harmlessly inward above the guitarist's head. For all of this to be just a momentary startlement, one more fleeting weirdness of city life that she can tell me about when she arrives home, fifteen or twenty minutes later.

I scan the faces of the pedestrians, the guitarist, the shop clerk slumped on his stool. *There must be something*, I think, *that one of you can do*.

Five steps beyond the guitarist, Angela stops on the sidewalk, her right leg extended before her, and looks back at him. Turns, of course, and retraces her steps, the white oval fading in to condemn her as always.

Press pause. Angela frozen now, circled, marked. The faintest suggestion of Angela, really: this single frame's array of pixels, plucked from the context of before and after, barely sufficient to convey a sense of her at all. Move your eyes close enough to the screen and she seems to be flying apart.

Lean back in the chair. Exhale, think a moment, reach for the side of the laptop. It's wrong to leave her suspended this way, half-formed, half-dissolved, a second away from becoming nothing at all. That white oval trapping her, marking her out from the world.

Press power. Stand, stretch. Time to feed the dog.

* * *

I meet Angela's mother, awkwardly, when she comes to the apartment to retrieve what she will refer to, twice during the course of our afternoon together, as Angela's "estate." Her name is Doris, and I realize I hadn't known that fact until today. I offer her my fumbling condolences in the doorway; she offers me none in return. I can't find it in me to take offense. How else should she react to meeting this interloper, this man who knew her daughter less than half a year, who lived with her for only half of that? Part of me wants to assure her that we loved one another, that so far as I know, Angela was happy at the end, but there seems no point. This woman's memories of Angela begin before her birth, encompass her existence from end to end. She has the overwhelmingly greater claim to grief, and would gain nothing at all by understanding mine.

We move quietly and methodically, not quite together, through the two small rooms of the apartment, emptying drawers and closets, boxing up a life. In Angela's nightstand, I come across a jumbled array of random objects, little totems whose significance I will never, now, have any chance to learn: a laminated bus pass printed in a foreign alphabet; a photo of Angela on a beach beside a dark-haired man whose name I have no way of guessing; a thin gold necklace strung through a turquoise pendant in the shape of a bird. Drink coasters and matchbooks printed with the names of places she visited before I knew her. I transfer these items into a large ziplock baggie, seal it shut, place it gently on top of a stack of sweaters inside one of the open boxes.

For ninety minutes we move furniture out into the hallway, down the two flights of stairs, out into the small rental truck that Doris has parked in the loading zone outside the building. Remaining in the front room, afterward: the desk that my laptop sits on beneath the window, and my single chair, surrounded by all the boxes we have yet to carry down. In the bedroom, only the bed and a few piles of my clothes lying here and there. Angela's mother steps through the doorway and looks down at the bed. "The bedframe came from her grandmother," she says.

I nod and strip off the blanket and the pale-blue sheets, pull the mattress and the box springs off the frame, prop them against the side wall. The sheets and the blanket disappear into yet another box. Doris produces a black marker from the front pocket of her jeans and writes "STEAM CLEAN" carefully across its lid. We disassemble the bedframe and carry it down to the truck, piece by piece. Back upstairs, when I reach for the mattress leaning against the box springs, Doris looks at them and looks at me. I see the quick flicker of distaste that crosses her face. "I'm not sure what anyone would want to do with those," she says.

I leave them propped against the wall, and we begin packing up toothbrushes and towels in the bathroom. Then silverware, pots and plates in the kitchen. A vase that once held yellow flowers, empty now. Box after box goes down the stairs and into the truck. Throughout the afternoon, Doris exhibits not so much as a passing interest in Max, Angela's dog, as he watches our comings and goings, and so I inherit him without a word being spoken about it.

When all is done, after we've closed and locked the truck, I ask her about funeral arrangements.

"She wanted cremation," Doris says. "Not this soon, of course, but…" She looks away from me, across the street. "She didn't want a grave. Thought it was wasteful." I nod. That sounds like Angela. Doris is running the tip of her thumb along the teeth of the truck key in her left hand, up and down, up and down. "We'll scatter her ashes," she says.

I have only a vague and partial idea of who "we" might be, in this context, but there's no doubt that it isn't intended to include me. I say my farewells, render my useless apologies one last time, watch Angela's mother climb into the cab of her little truck and drive away.

* * *

The apartment nearly empty now, echoing every time I take a step. Cross the room to the laptop. Press play.

The dark, low car flickers past the shop window from left to right; the guitarist strums; Angela appears. Again, that downward, curious cast of her head; that particular way she dodges around the open guitar case, like the movements of some dance she's practiced all her life. The ache I feel as I watch her repeat these nine unyielding steps toward annihilation feels, on some level, unearned. After only six months, to be this consumed, this broken? It seems unworthy. Seven months ago, I hadn't known she existed at all. It's said that a person can't fall in love so quickly, not truly, not in any way that might stand the test of time, and some part of me has always believed that. Some other part of me ceased to believe it, the day I met her.

It's an academic question, though. In our case, there will be no test of time.

Angela stops on the screen, looks back toward the guitarist, swivels around to face him as she always does, one hand reaching toward her purse. The scatter of people around her trace out their individual paths, oblivious. The guitarist strums. The clerk flips a page in his book. I sit before this screen on a different block on a different day and wait for the floating oval to enclose her. *There must be something*, I think, *that one of us can do.*

* * *

I've taken to walking Max down the block where it happened, always on the opposite side of the street: closer to the viewpoint of the camera that shot the video, farther from the actual succession of sights that proved to be Angela's last. I can't bring myself to walk up to the doorway of the candle shop and look into it, to imagine that utterly vacant and unremarkable square of concrete being the last thing she would ever see. Even from across the street, I can grasp its insufficiency for that purpose, its lack of any quality at all that might have pleased her eyes. I try to remind myself that there are other senses, other stimuli, any number of things that the video couldn't have captured or conveyed. Perhaps the smell of the candles, or the feel of the sunlight on her skin? It *was* sunny, in the video. Surely there would have been something, some passing, pleasant sensation that might have made the end a tiny bit worthwhile, helped to make it bearable as the end?

I think of the guitarist, the music he played that caught at her and drew her back. Here, away from the endlessly-looping video, outside in this world that continues on in more than two dimensions, I hope his song was beautiful. I hope it was the sweetest sound she ever heard.

* * *

Press play.

I've wondered from time to time about the provenance of this video: how it made its way from the back of the convenience store out onto the web, who took the time and care to position that floating oval around Angela's image in the raw footage. None of the cursory local news articles that appeared after the shooting had a copy of the video embedded. The police would have reviewed the footage for evidence, presumably, but the video doesn't appear anywhere on their departmental account. Things like this just leak out, I suppose, although the mechanics of how that happens have always puzzled me. The YouTube page which contains the video offers me no hints. The poster was someone who goes by the name "archon11." He has no bio, no avatar, no contact information of any kind. This is the only video in his stream. It's as if he appeared in the world for the sole purpose of communicating this one, unpleasant piece of information, then vanished from the Earth, his task completed.

Press replay.

It's hard to tell whether archon11's motives in posting the video were lurid or sympathetic. The title he's assigned to it reads *womman shot on sidewalk LOOK CLOSELY*, which seems to suggest the former. Part of me wonders if he's getting a cut of the money from the dog food ads. But in the description field beneath it, he has written, simply: *this need to change.*

So far, this page has been blessedly free of the internet harassers who make it their hobby to troll the grieving. It has attracted no comments, no likes or dislikes, no apparent attention from the rest of the world at all. I've begun to suspect, with some embarrassment, that the video's now-sizable and growing view count might reflect precisely the number of times I've played and replayed it over the past weeks, searching for some clue I can't articulate to a problem with no conceivable solution. I recognize that my decision-making has become impaired these days, that I'm having trouble with the mechanics of daily living. I've meant to go visit the little storage space that I rented when I first moved in here with Angela, bring some of my own furniture back to the apartment, at least dig out some sheets and pillows to put over the bare mattress and box springs that are now the only contents of the bedroom. I've meant to call the landlord, see about changing the joint lease to be in my name only, make sure that no further rent payments will be deducted from Angela's bank account, if it still exists. I've meant to call in to work. I took time off after the shooting, but I haven't been keeping track of the days. Probably my officially-sanctioned mourning period has ended, and I was meant to have been back there by now. My phone has been dead for days, though. Doris apparently boxed up my phone charger by mistake while we were clearing out the bedroom and took it with her, and I haven't taken the time to buy a replacement for that, either.

Objectively, I know that my failure to do these things ought to worry me. I tell myself that I should stand up now, step away from the laptop, leave the apartment for a while, but I'll be doing that later anyway, when I walk Max. My responsibilities to him, I discharge faithfully, as Angela would have wanted. What she might have wanted for me, I prefer not to dwell on.

Press replay. Sit through the ad for dog food. Watch Angela walk and turn and die again.

* * *

Just after sunset, rounding the corner with Max in tow, starting down our now-accustomed path along the sidewalk that leads past the convenience store, I hear music from across the street, the strumming of a single guitar. I recognize the man playing it. A moment of unreality, like time looping back on itself: He's seated in that same spot beneath the window of the candle shop, wearing what might well be the same clothes, his guitar case lying open on the sidewalk beside him.

I pause, and then, for the first time, I cross over to the opposite sidewalk. I fight the urge to turn and run as I make my way down toward him, his guitar case and extended leg the only things cutting across the diagonal lines of the sidewalk as they dwindle and converge in the distance. This, more or less, is what Angela saw, what she heard as she took her final steps toward oblivion. This was all there was for her. I look around, but there's little for the eye to settle on. Some apartment windows above me, the sky in the distance. Her sky would have been different, brighter, but mine is pretty tonight.

Drawing closer, the music clearer. The guitarist is, in fact, quite good, his head bowed and bobbing lightly as he picks out the chords of some intricate instrumental ballad that I feel I ought to recognize. I guide Max around the edge of his open guitar case, a thin scattering of coins and a single crumpled dollar bill visible inside it, and study what I can see of his face as we walk by. Weathered skin, a lean nose, hair hanging to his shoulders. His jacket is a dark, faded blue. I've seen it in the video, hundreds of times now, but I hadn't known that detail about it. It's strange, seeing him in color.

Just beyond where he's sitting lies the alcove containing the candle shop's doorway. Angela's resting place. I slow down but don't stop, looking at it only sideways, in passing, as she might have done. It's entirely empty: no doormats, no planters, no ceramic cats, just this flat, blank square of nothing. Some dim stains visible on the concrete, but they're well away from the spot where she fell, toward the back of the alcove along the right-hand wall, more likely the product of rainwater than blood. Max shows no reaction as we pass by, doesn't seem to smell her here. I'm relieved by that. Take another step, and another. Somewhere over to my right, the camera mounted on the convenience-store wall, recording all of this for no one's benefit. Ahead of me, only more sidewalk, very much like the stretch I'm on now. The guitarist playing more slowly at my back as his song works its way around to a leisurely finale.

I'd meant to just pass by, to see him and hear him once and move on, but I find myself slowing at this point, turning, retracing my steps. I stop beside the open doorway and wait for him to finish playing. It's not lost on me whose path I've just reenacted; I imagine a floating white oval appearing ghostly in the air above the sidewalk to my left, encircling me, sending its signal to the universe: *Take this one.* No shots ring out this evening, nothing changes. A dark-colored car eases past us on the street, low to the ground, the thrum of its engine mingling with the guitar chords for a moment and fading as it pulls away.

The guitarist holds a last, quavering, sustained note, and then his hands go still. He looks up and smiles. Wide eyes, clear. Deep seams in the skin around them. "I like your dog, man," he says. He extends his left hand, and Max trots a couple steps closer, sniffs it, presses his nose against his fingers. The guitarist makes a few low noises, scratches Max's ears. The elements of his face are an odd mixture of youth and age: either he's older than he looks, or he looks older than he is. Max circles back around toward my legs after a moment, and the guitarist returns his left hand to the neck of his guitar, raises the pick in his right, preparing to play again.

"Do you mind if I interrupt you for a minute?" I say. "I want to talk to you about the woman who got shot here the other week."

A strange expression enters his eyes, pained but guarded. "Yeah, that was a bad deal," he says slowly. "Real bad deal." He lowers his right hand, resting it against the strings. "Did you know her?"

"Yeah. She was my…" I want to say *my love*, but I can imagine it sounding forced, pretentious if spoken aloud, and so in this small, sad way known to no one but me, I cheapen her. "…my girlfriend."

The guitarist nods. "I had a feeling," he says, "her people were going to be along at some point."

This is a strange thought for me to consider. Apart from myself and Doris, I barely know who her people are. "Why's that?"

He shrugs. "She died right next to me. Right there where you're standing. Shit, I'm practically the one who killed her. I figured there was going to be a reckoning, sooner or later. And here you are."

I'm completely at a loss now. "Did you…? Wait. Did you know the guy who shot her?"

"Never saw him. Cops said they didn't think he was aiming at us. No, it was just…"

I stay quiet, let him find the words.

"I keep my head down while I'm playing. My line of work, people get uncomfortable if you look at them too much. But I see who's around me. Who's walking past me, who's slowing down, who's maybe going to stop and listen for a bit. I saw her walk by. She was real pretty. Just so pretty. She went past, and then I see her turning around, coming back, I could tell she was going to throw a tip in. Then, just, boom. She's down on the ground there, people are screaming. I was going to help her, you know, but her head was just…" He breaks off, looks up. "Sorry. You don't want to hear about that."

"It's okay," I say. "I'm sure you didn't want to see it."

"No," he says. "No, I didn't. And ever since then, I just keep…replaying it, you know? She turned around and came back because of me. If she hadn't done that… Shit, even if I'd just been sitting ten more feet up the block, then maybe she'd still be—"

"I know what you mean." It's never occurred to me that he might be burdened with these thoughts as well. It's never truly occurred to me that he existed at all, outside of those 26 seconds of video.

"And she seemed nice. Maybe I shouldn't say that, it's not like I knew her, but you'd know. Yeah?"

"Oh, yeah. She was…" And there my voice leaves me. *She was.* The other words won't come, none that could do her justice. The hardest things in the world to make someone feel are other people's happiness and other people's sadness. How do you convey the experience of finding her at last, of finding that she will have you? How do you describe the way it feels when this life you've simply been drifting through for years is suddenly set right, when you know without doubt that your arrival has done the same for hers, when you both begin to inhabit this unaccustomed but entirely correct new *us* that seems to confirm everything you've ever daydreamed about but never actually believed in, when you feel that the world is finally, for the first time, for this little while, working as intended, the keys to the kingdom in both your hands, and then for no reason that anyone can give you it flips back around and it's all snatched away and nothing that she was will ever be again and goddamn it, goddamn it, goddamn it Angela why of all possible or impossible things in the world did they have to end you?

"Hey, I'm sorry, man," the guitarist says softly. Some of this is showing on my face, apparently.

"It's all right," I say, turning my head away from him. "It's all right."

He waits, until I'm able to look at him again. "I haven't come back here since it happened. Been staying away from this whole neighborhood, pretty much. But this afternoon, I felt like I ought to come out here and play for her. It's been three weeks today."

"Has it?" I really have lost track of time.

"Yeah. And I kind of have these beliefs about the number three. Like if you want something to happen, and you say it three times..."

Please don't, I think. *Please don't say something mystical and asinine just when I'm starting to like you.*

"...that's usually the most powerful. Or, like, when I put my seed money into my case, I always put in three of each kind of coin, and three dollar bills. I always have the best days if I do that." He glances into the guitar case. "Except I had to spend a couple of them today, so..." He looks back at me, sees that he's not getting any uptake on this. "Anyway, that's why I came out. I've been feeling so fucking bad about this. But now you know. You want to hate me, you want to yell at me, you want to beat my ass, whatever it is, I understand."

I shake my head. "You dropped your guitar..."

He looks down at his lap. "What?"

"When they shot her." I can see the scratches and gouges in the wood along the guitar's base, where it rests against the leg of his jeans, little fragments torn from its edges as it slid along the concrete. "I mean, that's your livelihood, right? I'm sure you take good care of it. But when you saw she was hurt, you just went to her. Didn't set it down, didn't put it in its case. Just dumped it, let it skid. Tried to help her. There's no way I could be mad at you."

This is only half a lie. I've hated his image in the video, blamed him for her death a thousand times, wished desperately that the bullet could have missed her and entered him instead. But it's not the same, in person. I've heard him play. I know why Angela turned back. What I'm telling him, now, is true now.

The guitarist lets out a long breath. "I'm glad to hear you say that," he says. Then I see his head turn. "How did you know about all that? Were you here when she——?"

"There's a video of it online." I find myself speaking carefully now; some confession I don't quite want to make. This new species of shame, the fear that someone else might glimpse the thing you're becoming. I gesture toward the convenience store. "Security camera over there recorded it. Somebody stuck it up on YouTube. So I looked at it once, you know? Right after it happened. I had to see."

"Jesus. I can't imagine. Are they really allowed to do that?"

I shrug, powerless, as I am in every aspect of this. "I don't even know who 'they' is. Someone just posted it."

"That is fucked up," the guitarist says. "I swear, man, if there'd been anything I could have done for her..."

"I know." I see him playing out the same sequence of motions, over and over, his hands reaching out to her and stopping, wanting to comfort her but seeing that there's no point. I see Angela slowing and turning and dying upon this spot, again and again, with no recourse, not even a chance to wonder why. I see myself sitting before a laptop in an empty apartment day after day, watching the video, watching the video, watching the video. "We do what we do," I say. "We just do. Nothing changes it."

The guitarist looks off toward the pink and orange of the sunset. "I always figured we had, like, angels, you know? Spirits looking out for us. Something went wrong, they'd come along and make it right. I've been asking myself why that didn't happen."

"I guess hers was busy that day." I don't want to have this conversation with him, especially don't want it to work around to that place where I'll be told that from a certain, broader perspective, this might all be for the best. It isn't. No part of this is better than any imaginable alternative. I tighten my grip on Max's leash, fish into my pocket with my free hand, find only a penny and a ten-dollar bill there. Fuck it. I lean over and set them both down inside the guitar case. "Thanks for talking with me. I'll let you get back to it."

"Oh, hey, man. I can't take that."

"It's from her," I say. "She wanted to give you something. She never got a chance to."

He glances back into the dark of the alcove, shakes his head. "What was her name, anyway?"

It's been a while since I said it out loud. "Angela."

I see his lips repeat it, silently. "You were a lucky man."

"I was," I say, and then I turn and lead Max away from him, down toward the sections of the sidewalk that Angela never reached.

* * *

Press play.

One detail about the video has begun to trouble me, something that went unnoticed until my eyes and my mind had absorbed a thousand replays. In the very first frame, that dark, low-slung car is already halfway into view, passing across the scene from left to right. Then Angela appears, walks, turns, dies, the white oval fading in and fading out around her. The guitarist scrambles across the sidewalk to help her, reaches out to cradle her head but doesn't. And just before the video ends, a dark, low-slung car appears, moving from left to right, emerging exactly halfway into view at the moment when we freeze on the final frame.

The problem I'm having is that it appears to be the same car, both times, entering the frame once at the beginning of the video and entering it again at the end.

Press replay. Dog food ad. Curse, fume, fidget until it's over. Then lean very close to the laptop and look at the screen, look closely.

The car is oddly shaped, some make and model I don't recognize. Its windows partly tinted, the driver only a broad, vague silhouette inside. Memorize its shape, its size, its placement upon the road. Watch it pass by. Then wait for 23 more seconds, while the clerk reads and the guitarist plays and Angela dies before she ever starts to fall. Ignore all of that for the moment and focus on this spot, here in the lower left, until that dark blur of entering motion begins again. Yes. The same odd, low shape, the same broad silhouette behind the wheel.

Video ends. Press replay. When it starts again, press pause immediately, finger stabbing down, freezing on this first frame, the car already halfway into view. Take a screenshot of this. Save it.

Press play. Wait, breath held, finger poised, till we reach the other end. A hint of motion in the lower left. Press pause. Too soon: the video frozen a couple of frames too early, only the car's front bumper visible as yet. Press play and press pause, press play and press pause, advancing a frame at a time until the car has half emerged in the final frame. Screenshot. Save it. It's the same car, definitely the same car.

And that's not possible. I know this block, both sides of it now. I've walked its length a dozen times, out with Max. It's long, lined with storefronts from end to end. No alleys, no turnings, no way for a driver to circle back outside the view of the camera. You'd have to go all the way down to the corner, turn left or right and drive to the next street over, circle back around the entire length of the block in order to drive into the frame again from the same direction. No matter how fast your car, how light the traffic, there's simply no way someone could accomplish that in the span of twenty-three seconds. And yet it is the same car, both times. Isn't it?

Open both screenshots, the first frame and the last, each in its own window. Lay them directly above one another. Focus on the first shot, then flip to the second. Back to the first, back to the second. Everything else within the frame shifts a little during these transitions, the people most noticeably, of course: the clerk is reading his book in the first shot and looking out the window in the second; the guitarist is playing in the first shot and kneeling over Angela in the second; Angela is absent in the first shot and lying dead in the doorway in the second. But the car... Not only is it the same car, with the same driver, but it's in exactly the same position in both shots. Flip between the first frame and the last frame, and it doesn't appear to have moved at all. As if time had looped back around and begun a second iteration, for this car and this driver alone.

Zoom in on the lower left corners of both screenshots, by exactly the same amount. Flip between them. Flip back. It's not just that the car is in the same place: I'm increasingly convinced that I'm looking at the exact same image. Zoom in further, until both images of the car begin to fray and pixelate. Flip to the first screenshot. Flip to the second. Again, again. Even the empty areas of the street in the background change ever-so-slightly between the two images – light shifting imperceptibly on the pavement, video noise yielding a different pattern of grain – but within the body of the car itself, every pixel is identical.

Back to the video. Press play. Watch it from end to end, until it freezes once more on this final image. My eyes remain convinced, seeing it: The front end of this car, impossible but obstinately there, its dark mark across the lower corner of the frame like an artist's signature.

Lean back. Ponder this.

I've known all along that this video isn't in its original form. Someone added the white oval to it, somewhere along the line, to call attention to Angela as she walked and fell. Did they alter this, too? Edit the image of this car in for a second, faked appearance in the closing frames? It seems so. But what possible motivation could anyone have for doing that?

My knowledge of video editing is sketchy at best. I decide to learn more. For the first time in a very long time, I open a new tab in my browser, one that doesn't show Angela dying. I'll go to Google, poke around, see what comes to light.

Typing "video editing" into the search box brings back millions of results: how-to articles, software ads, job listings. Pure noise, from my perspective. I start adding other keywords: "oval," "circle," "fake," "tampering." Skim through websites, images, other videos that have circles and ovals drawn around objects within them, sometimes white, sometimes yellow, sometimes blue. A video of a man crashing a skateboard into a fountain, in the background of some politician's speech; a math tutorial about how to calculate the area of an ellipse. I don't feel like I'm getting anywhere, perhaps because I don't know what I'm looking for. Go back to the tab containing the video of Angela. Press play. Watch until the oval fades in and then press pause, freeze it, study it. Look closely. The inner ring of the oval is a line of pure white, fading toward transparency at its outer edges, with a distinctive gradient unlike the ovals in any of the other videos I've seen in my search results. Does this matter? I have no idea.

Back to Google. Select image search. Type "video edit oval" and just scroll, scroll, scroll, scroll, looking at everything that goes by. Nothing catches my eye. Switch to video search. Same keywords. Scroll, scroll…

Here. A preview image for a video which shows a partial view of a football field, filmed at an angle from above. One of the players in the image has an oval enclosing him. *This* oval, the white inner ring, fading out around the edges. Click the link, which leads to a different page on YouTube. *Miracle touchdown saves Highland boys' postseason streak*, reads the title. Press play. Opposing lines of football players rush together, collide and contend. Red shirts shoving against blue shirts. Ignore them, wait for an oval to appear. There, encircling one red-shirted player as he breaks free of the moving mass. Press pause.

The same oval, floating above his image. A little shorter, a little broader than the one which encloses Angela as she dies, but almost certainly produced by the same software. Read the description below the video.

Astonishing last-second touchdown catch by Holman. Must see this to believe it.

Final score, 13–12.

Edited with Reality Plus.

Press play. The white oval tracks the player in the red shirt for a few seconds as he darts around the shoving bodies and sprints toward the end zone. A larger member of the opposing team peels off and charges after him, surprisingly fast for his size, the camera panning to follow them both. The white oval fades away, just the two of them on the screen now. The football flies into view from above, thrown from somewhere within the churning mass they've left behind. The red-shirted player jumps several feet into the air as he crosses the line of the end zone, wraps his fingers around the falling ball, and at that instant, the player in blue smashes into him from behind. The player in the red shirt cartwheels violently, spins through two full revolutions in mid-air, hits the ground head-first so hard and at so grotesque an angle that I'm certain the impact has killed him. His body tumbles across the turf and flops to a limp halt, curled onto his side. The camera zooms in. He lies perfectly still. The player who hit him circles back, drops to one knee beside him, a look of horror plainly visible on his face. Then, without moving any other part of his body, the red-shirted player raises his right arm, holding up the football. The video ends, frozen on this image.

What can this tell me? The same editing software that someone employed to mark up the footage of Angela's death was also used to superimpose a white oval on the video of some high-schooler's game-winning moment. So what? Other people's happy endings are of little use to me now.

One last breadcrumb to follow, while I'm here. Back to the search box. Type "reality plus." Just keep following the trail, for lack of anything better to do. I learn that a piece of software named Reality Plus does indeed exist, a tool so obscure that its own website ranks only fourth in the results of a search for its own name. Some of the links around it contain snippets of reviews. *Reality Plus is a lifesaver! Highly recommended!* Immediately below that: *Unusable. Crashes constantly.* I click on the link to the main website, and land upon what is possibly the most bare-bones, low-effort web page I've ever seen. No graphics, no testimonials, no screenshots of this software in action. Just an empty white page containing a few lines of unformatted black text:

Reality Plus.

Is editor for makking the necessary changes large and small. People ask is good, is not good, no matter. Serve its purpose. You encounter problem, mistake, thing not as it should be? Good news, all is opensource! Don't like what you are seeing, fix it. :)

Below that are two links, reading *Download editor* and *Download source code.* Click on the first one. Save an installer program with a meaningless string of numbers for a name. Run it. A security warning pops up, reminding me of the risks of malware, trojans, viruses. I think about those risks and decide that I don't care about them in the slightest. Press approve. Wait while the installer does whatever it does. Finished. Run it.

The window that finally opens is ringed on three sides by collections of tiny buttons whose icons convey nothing to me. An empty workspace area in the middle, marked by pink, misaligned text which reads *Import video.* I click at random through an enormous set of menu items, just looking at their names. *Select region. Lasso select. Reverse select. Copy. Copy layer. Collapse layer. Lighten. Darken. Blend. Blur.* I locate what appear to be options for inserting an oval-shaped marker into a frame of video, placing it, resizing it. I find a submenu marked *Advanced options,* filled with the names of tasks I can't even comprehend.

Looking into the void of this empty workspace, I reach a dead end. Yes, I'm convinced that this software was used to add the floating oval to Angela's video. I'm convinced that a proficient user could also have used it to doctor in an extra image of a car, copy some pixels from the first frames into the last ones to make it look as if it had driven by twice. I'm not the least bit closer to being able to imagine why.

Close the Reality Plus window. Close this unaccustomed extra tab in my browser and return to the page containing the video of Angela. Back to the world I know.

Press play. The guitarist strums. The clerk reads. Angela turns back and falls, as always.

* * *

Mid-morning on the sidewalk across from the candle shop. No guitarist seated over there today. Max has run out of dog food. I tie his leash to one end of the bike rack in front of the convenience store and step inside it for the first time.

Having seen the shop's interior only in muted, shaded black and white, the brightness of the lights inside, the array of primary colors on the shelves, comes as an almost physical shock. It takes me a few seconds to sort it all out, to begin to recognize the place again. The clerk behind the counter is the one from the video, a young man with dark eyes and a deep black beard. Mounted on a bracket high on the rear wall: the beige oblong of the security camera, looking down on me with its ever-hungry eye.

Go straight to the pet food section. I've never been in the shop, but I know exactly where it is. The convenience store carries two types of dog food. One of them is the brand that's been advertised to me incessantly, day in, day out, all these weeks of replaying the video. I pick up a bag of the other brand and carry it to the counter. Little victories.

Study the clerk as he rings up my purchase. Bored, barely looking up from his book. I glance at the security camera watching over us, then back at the clerk. He'd have access to the back room, to whatever device this camera's footage feeds into. "I have kind of a weird question for you," I say.

"There are no weird questions, only weird answers," he says. "And I'll do my best to come through for you on that front."

Shit. The first part of my question, I suspect, has just been answered. I'd hoped he might speak with an accent, show some traces of mangled syntax that would align with my admittedly very small sample of archon11's writing style. Nothing of the sort, and he apparently spends entire workdays with his nose in books. Even after hearing him speak two sentences, it's hard for me to imagine him misspelling the word "woman," mixing up singular and plural verb forms. The clerk flips a page, continues reading, waiting for me to speak or go away.

"My girlfriend got shot right over there," I say, pointing across the street. "About three weeks back."

"Oh…" The clerk looks up, sets his book down. "Wow. Sorry. Yeah, I was here when that happened."

"I know," I say. "You were reading then, too." His eyes narrow. It's the reaction I was hoping for; I have his full attention now. "Your security camera up there recorded it. A section of the video got posted online. I'm guessing somebody who works here probably did that?"

The look of surprise on the clerk's face doesn't seem feigned to me. He shakes his head. "It's just me and my dad in here. I don't think he'd even know how. Anyway, the guy erased all the footage, so even if I'd wanted to do something like that…"

"What guy?"

The clerk shrugs. "Just this guy. Came in a few minutes after the shooting. Big, bald, button-up shirt, one of those kind of guys? He just strolls in, points up at the camera, goes, 'Need to see video.' I'm like, 'Yeah, who the fuck are you?' But he just keeps smiling at me, pointing. 'Need to see video. Need to see video.'"

I'm noticing that while the clerk has no accent himself, he mimics one subconsciously each time he quotes the other man.

"I was going to tell him to fuck off and go get a warrant, but then my dad comes out from the back, he's all like, 'No, no, come in, come in.' So we take him in the back. My dad thought he might be a cop." The clerk shakes his head. "Dude barely spoke English. He wasn't a cop. It was weird."

"What happened with him?"

"We bring him back to the office, I queue up the footage for him, and he's all, like, 'Yes, is good, leave now.' So we did."

"You just left him alone in your office? Why?"

"You've got to understand, where my dad's from, if someone with authority shows up, you don't say no to them. You might lie your ass off, but you never say no."

"But…what authority?"

The clerk spreads his hands, looking puzzled by this himself. "Just the way that he was. Like he was going to get everything he wanted from you anyway, so it was easier to get out of his way. You just didn't feel like arguing with him."

"Do you think he might have been the one who shot her?"

"I wondered about that. But I don't know. There were like five cop cars out on the street when he came in. He didn't seem tense. Wasn't in a hurry at all. Wasn't even scary, really. Just…persuasive."

"But once he was alone back there, he erased the footage?"

The clerk nods. "I went back there a couple hours later, tried to look at it myself. I was curious, I admit it. Like you said, I was reading when that all went down. I didn't actually see it happen. Thought I'd check it out. I know, dick move, my bad." I say nothing. I'm hardly in a position to throw stones on that point. "Anyway, the footage gets saved in these two-hour-long chunks. I opened up the one for those two hours, and it was just black. The whole way through, all two hours of it, just black. I mean, I could see if he'd just deleted it and walked out, but I don't know how the hell he turned the whole thing black."

"Edited it," I say.

"Something. Oh, and the police finally did come by, like three hours after that. Asked us if they could look at the video, too. They were pissed when we told them. Gave my dad all kinds of shit about it. Like it's his job to do their job, right? Trust me, all these questions you're asking me, they already asked us. Got a description of the guy, the whole deal."

"I'm not trying to point any fingers," I say. "I just want to talk to whoever put it online."

"It's seriously up there?" the clerk says. "Like, what would I search for if I wanted to watch it?"

"I really wish you wouldn't," I say, and hold his eyes until he takes my point.

"I hear you. So did the cops ever find this guy? Find anybody?"

"Not that I've heard of." It occurs to me that if they had, I might not know. Aside from that first evening, when the two detectives knocked on the door of the apartment to break the news to me, several hours after the fact, all their communication has been with Doris. I'm a footnote in all this, an afterthought, no relation to Angela. And I haven't been keeping up with the local news.

I've wondered, at times, why the gunman hasn't been more on my mind: trying to learn his identity, ensure that he's caught, satisfy myself that he'll be suitably punished. Perhaps because, if all that happens, Angela will be no less dead? Or perhaps the video itself has affected the way I see the world. Would I feel differently if the camera had captured him, too, if I'd been watching him raise the gun and pull the trigger day after day? Probably. This clerk, the guitarist, the driver of the black car, are real to me. I can see them, I can watch their movements, analyze their reactions. The gunman is an abstraction, an external force, a mere cause which impels the events I see to unfold in a specific sequence. Like time, like gravity. I rarely think of him. Strange that the arbitrary limits of what a camera sees, or doesn't, should have such power to shape things, to determine what seems contingent and what seems absolute.

"I hope they get him," the clerk says.

"Me too," I say, as I'm expected to, and pick up my bag of dog food.

I head back out to the sidewalk where Max is waiting. Someone's chained a bicycle to the rack beside him while I was in the shop. I kneel on the concrete next to its rear tire and untie his leash. A car eases past us on the street from left to right, accelerates. I look up at it, through the radiating lines of the bicycle's spokes. Low-slung, black paint job, tinted windows. Oddly shaped, a make and model that I've never seen anywhere, except twice every time I've ever watched the video, once at the beginning and once at the end. I scramble to my feet, staring after the car as it pulls away from me. I take a step in that direction, fumble the loop at the end of Max's leash around one handlebar of the bicycle, leave him there, begin to run.

Red light at the end of the block, the car slowing as it nears the corner. I speed up, my mind and muscles only gradually impressing upon me that my body is off-balance: the bag of dog food, forgotten, jostling in my right hand. No time to stop and set it down now. I tuck it in tight under my arm, lower my shoulders and run faster. Swerve past two middle-aged women walking toward me hand in hand, veer in the other direction to avoid a man in a white apron smoking a cigarette against the wall outside a diner. Nearly to the corner now. The light turns green, the car begins to pull forward. Sprint all-out across this last stretch of concrete, dodge around the hydrant at the end of the block, stumble out into the road directly in front of the black car's bumper, my left arm upraised, the right one still holding the dog food. "Stop, stop, stop!"

Brakes engaging, the car's front end dipping abruptly as it comes to a halt just shy of my knees. My left hand dropping onto the hood then, resting there, my chest heaving. Sitting at my laptop all day, every day for weeks has done my body no favors. I look at the driver through the windshield: a hairless head; curious, impassive eyes regarding me. "I need to talk to you," I say.

The driver's door opening, the hood of the car rising half an inch beneath my fingers as he steps out. He doesn't hurry, nor does he move slowly: just seems to flow from place to place and become still again in a new position. He's broadly-built, not particularly tall, dressed in slacks and a crisp shirt. His face forgettable. He could be a mid-level marketing executive at one of the tech companies downtown. He could be anyone.

"There was a shooting," I say. "Right up the block there." He's shaking his head, a faint, patient smile barely visible on his face. "You know what I'm talking about. You posted a video of it. Why?"

"I'm not good," he says.

"What?"

"The language…" He shakes his head again. "I'm not good. I can't help you." His accent, like his car, reminds me of nothing I've ever encountered. He begins to turn away.

"Archon eleven," I say, and he pauses, turns back to me. "That's you. Yes? You took the video from the store. You put it online. But you changed it first. You faked something. Made your car drive by a second time, after she died. I want to know why."

"Fake? No," he says. "I drive by, gun shoot, she fall. I want to drive by again, see that she get help she need. I drive by again."

"Then how'd you get around the block so fast? There's no possible way—"

He backs away from me, toward the open car door, raising his hands at either side. "I've done all I can for you," he says.

"I just want you to explain—"

Shaking his head again. "I'm not good. I've done all I can for you. You will understand this?"

Something about his presence, his manner, this benign, deflecting smile that stays fixed upon his face no matter what words he's saying or hearing, is utterly defeating. Dissuading. Sapping. I find myself mute, out of questions. He nods.

"You will understand."

He lowers himself back into his strange, low car, closes the door and drives away from me. I turn in a half circle on the pavement, watching him pass, watching the car recede, trying to remember what my other questions were. A horn honks nearby. I look around to see what it's honking at, only gradually understand that it's honking at me, the man standing in the middle of the street holding a bag of dog food. I retreat to the sidewalk, look off in the direction in which the black car has vanished, then start the long walk back up toward the convenience store to retrieve Max.

* * *

At home, I put the dog food into the cupboard, and realize that I've run out of food for myself as well. I kneel and open the cabinet beneath the kitchen sink. I've put this off, eaten every other scrap in the apartment first, but it's time. Inside the cabinet, at the back, sits an enormous cardboard pallet stacked with soup cans, wrapped in cloudy-looking plastic, never opened. Angela bought it one day before I moved in, scared by an article she'd read online about earthquakes, which recommended keeping a survival kit on hand. This was as far as she ever got with it. Her fears, as it turned out, should have focused on more mundane matters, on making it from one end of a block to the other. In any case, I tell myself, disaster has struck. I tear the plastic open, pull out a can of soup, heat it on the stove and make myself eat it.

Return to the laptop. Press play.

The black car drives into view, vanishes for 23 seconds while Angela walks and falls, then drives into view again. This couldn't possibly have happened, but its driver insists that it did, and my eyes still believe him.

Scan the page containing the video, look at the words he wrote here. *This need to change.* I can imagine his voice saying it, now, in that accent I've never heard anywhere else. I think of the barely-there web page for Reality Plus, that terse, garbled text that seemed almost reluctant to advertise its own product. *You encounter problem, mistake, thing not as it should be? Good news, all is opensource!* The same voice? I catch myself, draw back from the edge of that abyss. The internet is filled with anonymous people who express themselves poorly in English, and presumably in every other language as well. Don't start trying to draw meaningful lines between any arbitrary pair of such dots. Don't imagine that some guiding pattern has been laid out for you beneath the random chaos of life. That way, I'm certain, lies madness.

Press play. Watch Angela die.

Press replay. Watch Angela die.

Press replay. Watch Angela die, brought to you by this particular brand of dog food.

I begin to consider, with what I perceive to be an admirable degree of objectivity and clarity, whether madness would be any worse than this. The worst imaginable outcome has already happened. It's happening again on the screen, right now. Why, at this point, should I fear any alternative that might present itself?

There are no weird questions. Only weird answers.

I think of the football video I watched, the way its final few frames altered everything. If it had ended one second earlier, I would have been looking at footage of a horrific tragedy, a teenager lying dead in the dirt while another teenager who'd just killed him looked on in horror. Something as simple as an upraised arm holding a ball, a few pixels shifting on a screen, changes it into something else entirely. Those five or six frames of video, his body not even moving from where it landed, make the difference between him being a local, game-winning hero or lying in a hole in the ground.

Edited with Reality Plus.

There is the path of reason, and there is this path, equally clear before me, beckoning for me to follow it. What is the best-case scenario, if I don't? What is the worst-case scenario, if I do? It seems to me that they're exactly the same: I end up right here, where I am already.

Go to the desktop. Open Reality Plus. Spend ten minutes working out how to make it pull a video from a YouTube stream, save a local copy of it on my laptop. Copy the address from the browser, punch it in. Watch the indicators of progress flash by. *Downloading. Importing. Ready.* The empty workspace begins to fill with tiny images, every frame of the video laid out in sequence from end to end. Each of them a frozen instant, a connector in a logical progression which leads to the next moment and the next. And every one of them malleable, subject to revision with the proper tools.

All is open source.

These are my raw materials.

Don't like what you are seeing, fix it.

* * *

What changes to the circumstances of that afternoon would have kept Angela alive?

It's too open-ended a question, I soon realize, permitting an infinite number of answers. If she'd arrived on this block thirty minutes later, if she'd taken a different route on her way home, if she'd never left the apartment at all that day... All these answers are accurate, but unhelpful. I need something more narrowly tailored, something that will allow me to work with the materials I have. So: What circumstances would have allowed her to walk down this block, during these particular 26 seconds, and live?

I run through possible survival scenarios, working through the specifics of each one's aftermath with an eye toward greatest simplicity, least novelty. If she were merely standing in a different place when the gun fired, for example, then the bullet would strike the candle shop window instead and shatter it. Glass would need to fall; Angela would need to react to the sound of the shot, flinching and ducking and turning like all the others. She would also – I am certain of this – go over to check on the guitarist, make sure none of the broken glass had hit him. The guitarist himself would have to respond to these events with a completely new set of gestures, unlike any that the camera captured. The other pedestrians, once the initial shock had passed, might have noticed the broken window too, been drawn to go and look at it more closely. Too many new movements, too many extra details to get right. All of them, I suspect, beyond my skill to reproduce. Better if I can work as much as possible with elements that are already present in the early portions of the video, replicate and extend what exists with only the minimal changes required for verisimilitude. The people who are still should remain still; those who are moving should continue moving, in roughly the same manner as before. How to achieve that?

The camera never captured the shooter, never saw the gun. He's an abstraction, an external force, a mere cause. The video only depicts the consequences of his actions. Alter those consequences, remove their visible effects, and there would be no proof that he'd ever been there at all. The best and simplest solution, I conclude, is if the gun never fires, if every person present just keeps on doing what they were doing in the first place. Does the shooter's gun jam? Does *he* travel down a different block that afternoon? With something verging upon joy, I realize that it doesn't matter. He's not in the video anyway. I'm not obliged to explain his absence. All that matters is that the bullet never leaves the gun.

Let it be so.

I begin my work with the clerk, since of all the people present in the video, he moves the least. He will be my test case, my learning experience. My goal is simply to keep him seated here on his stool, his head bent over his book, from the opening frame of the video until the last one.

Accomplishing this takes me three full days. First I have to learn the new interface, gain an understanding of this tool's capabilities, its limitations, its arbitrary quirks. Figure out what all those buttons do. Then I have to become proficient at actually using them. Every single frame that I alter, during this early going, requires me to learn some new process, some additional technique to achieve the things I'm trying to accomplish: How to select and copy the region of pixels depicting the clerk in a given frame without picking up too much of his surroundings; how to maintain his body's precise position within the image when I paste those pixels into a later frame, so that he appears to remain perfectly still, continuing to read his book. And it's not just a matter of transferring the contents of an earlier frame into a later one: the existing image of the clerk in the later frame must be removed first; portions of the background that his figure was obscuring must be copied in and reconstructed from other frames as well, their seams stitched together, shadows and boundaries and noise smoothed out while still maintaining the overall grain of the video. All the new elements made to harmonize so well with the existing ones that the eye can't detect where a change occurred, can't convince itself that a change has been made at all. For every frame after the moment when the clerk first begins to lift his head, I do this. I hadn't fully appreciated, until now, just how many individual frames a 26-second video comprises.

Adding to my burden is the fact that, true to its anonymous reviewer's billing, Reality Plus freezes up and crashes, quite frequently. Open-source it may be, therefore fixable in theory, but the skills to correct this software's failings are entirely beyond me. This much, at least, I will have to live with, in exactly the form I've received it. I get into the habit of saving my work every time I've made the minutest increment of progress, lest I find myself staring at an empty desktop with an hour's or a day's changes undone.

I persevere, select and copy and paste and alter, slog on. It's like digging a tunnel under a mountain with a soup spoon, but eventually I do begin to progress. I find myself moving through the steps of the process a little more quickly, learning to more accurately predict the results of my decisions, developing a repeatable workflow. Despite all the setbacks I encounter, it's good to see something other than the browser every time I switch on my laptop, even if most of my waking moments are still spent looking at some portion or another of the video. I'm a participant now, shaping its events rather than passively accepting them. The feeling becomes addictive, euphoric. However slowly I move, I'm moving forward.

Twice a day, I force myself to stop what I'm doing, put a can of soup on the stove, feed Max while it's heating, and walk him after we've both eaten. We seldom travel as far from home as the block containing the convenience store anymore. That would eat up too much time, and there's much to be done here.

Very, very late on the third day, I declare my work on the clerk completed. I collapse upon the bare mattress in the bedroom, Max curling in to sleep beside me. Sunlight outside when I awaken. Return to the laptop. The guitarist is next on my to-do list, and he'll be more challenging than the clerk was. He moves more while he's seated, in the early frames before the gunshot – strumming hands and bobbing head that will need to continue their motions convincingly, all the way through to the end of the video – and he travels a greater distance in the later frames, obscuring several portions of sidewalk, wall and doorway which will need to be patched up, frame by frame, once I've deleted his kneeling figure from in front of them. Phase two of my task. Begin.

He's more challenging, yes, but I finish with him in half the time. Most of the lessons I've learned from the clerk carry over, albeit with some modifications to my methods to account for his greater complexity. He'll look seamless, in the finished work. I'm getting good at this.

On to the pedestrians now, a harder problem still. I'll need each of them to walk through portions of the frame that they never reached in the original video, and their movements will have to persuade. They'll pass behind objects and doorframes, need to be partially occluded by them. In some cases, they'll have to walk past one another, in places where they hadn't before, shifting on the sidewalk to make room. Their shadows will need to travel with them, conforming properly to all the vagaries of gratings, signposts, pebbles, potholes.

I have no idea how long I struggle with all this. Days, many of them. Weeks? More than one, certainly. Probably fewer than three. I can't measure the passage of time any more finely than that. Every hour, every frame, brings some new challenge to overcome, some unforeseen problem that must be worked around. The physics of walking, the way that shoes and human feet interact with concrete, is incredibly difficult to depict and sustain convincingly across uneven surfaces. The shadows, as I expected, are a nightmare. So many variables, so much trial and error, whole days' worth of work which must be discarded and begun anew because the movements I've produced simply don't look real.

During my walks with Max, I study the people around me: how their feet and legs and arms move, how their shadows alter, how they adjust their gait and balance to accommodate a curb cutting or an obstacle in their path. Some of the lessons I learn can be applied to the problem at hand. Most are worthless to me. My progress so terribly slow now, so halting. This sense of futility, of despair creeping in.

I force myself to take a break, to invest in a field trip a little farther from home. I return to the sidewalk across from the candle shop, take up position in front of the convenience store at the same hour of the afternoon when the video was recorded. I need to understand how people walk on *these* sidewalks, how their shadows behave in *this* light. Approximations and guesswork won't suffice. It has to be right, it has to ring true. I feel like I'm inching closer to an understanding, as I stand here and watch the people pass, watch them enter and leave the shop, but this vantage point still isn't quite

ideal. I move back and forth a few times in front of the shop
window, rise up on my toes, crane my neck, cover one eye to bring
my view a bit closer to what the camera would see. It's unfortunate
that I see in color rather than black-and-white, but I can't think of
any immediate solution to that problem. I'm also a bit too close to
the pedestrians. I wonder if I could talk my way to the rear of the
convenience store, borrow a chair or a stepladder to stand on, raise
my eyes to exactly the level of the camera and watch the street from
there until I get the viewing angle right.

The door behind me opens, and the bearded clerk steps out onto
the sidewalk. He fishes a pack of cigarettes from his shirt pocket,
holds one out to me. I shake my head absently. I've never smoked.
He puts the cigarette in his own mouth and lights it. A man in a
baseball cap walks past us, and I crouch a bit lower to study the way
he shifts course around our bodies, how his shadow throws two
narrow, darkened stripes along the horizontal rails of the bike rack.
This is useful, definitely useful. The clerk puffs on his cigarette,
exhales slowly, waits until my eyes leave the man's receding figure
and turn back to him. Eye contact comes as a faint shock. I haven't
looked anyone in the eye recently.

"Listen, I understand that you went through a hard time," the
clerk says – his use of the past tense in this regard making me want to
erupt in mad, sudden laughter – "but I need to ask you to stand
someplace else. You're worrying people. Maybe you could go to the
other side of the street for a while?"

I look across at the candle shop, the empty alcove. "There's
nothing over there," I say.

As I'm rounding the corner on my way back home, it occurs to
me that I should have accepted the cigarette from him. Merely
standing in one place on a sidewalk for long stretches of time does
strike people as odd, it's true. And yet, if you're holding a cigarette in
your hand while you do it, then it becomes acceptable behavior. Not
condoned, necessarily, but understood. Perhaps I can buy a pack of

them when I return to the shop tomorrow afternoon. Take another opportunity, while I do so, to study the clerk in his accustomed habitat, make sure my rendition of him is sound. I might even encounter his father instead, who from the sound of things is much easier to persuade. Find a pretext to browse along the rear wall of the shop first, gather some data there. Levering myself up onto the first or second shelf even for a few moments, just as someone walks by outside, should give me a clearer idea of how a person's shadow would look to the camera. Then go to the counter, buy the cigarettes, conduct more research out front. It won't be nearly as easy for them to send a paying customer away.

Home, door, laptop. Press power.

Zoom in on the shadows. Resume working. Resume failing.

* * *

That night, just as I'm beginning to fall asleep, I realize the solution to my shadow problem. I open my eyes and sit upright in the dark. I've had other ideas like this, on other nights, but this one feels right, seems to account for all the variables that have hindered my progress thus far. I hurry back out to the laptop in the front room, press power, re-open Reality Plus (which has crashed again during the minutes since I went to bed), and test my theory on one of the pedestrians in a few frames of the video. It's working. His shadow looks flawless. This method can be applied to all the others, too. I work for the next 18 hours.

When I return to the mattress and sleep at last, the pedestrians have joined the guitarist and the clerk on my list of tasks completed.

When I awaken, I turn my attention briefly to the low, black car. Its driver says he drove by a second time because of the gunshot. There will be no gunshot; therefore he need only drive by once. Remove the car from the closing frames of the video, leave them showing only empty street. This is child's play to me now, an hour's work at most. Press save. Eat soup. Feed Max.

And now, at the last, I come to Angela. Every trick I've learned, every skill I've honed must be brought to bear on her behalf, and they must not falter. Not one instant, one footfall, one pixel out of place. She'll be the one I look at most closely, the one whose every smallest action must convince. Start, then, from the moment she passes the candle shop doorway. Select, duplicate, extend. Keep her moving forward, frame by frame. Reality Plus has an option to play back the video at any time, but I never use it, only navigate from a single frame to the one before it or after it. Compare, assess, convince myself that her movements are flowing as they should, that the distance traveled from one frame to the next remains constant and believable.

Days and nights go by. I erase that white, enclosing oval from the world, restore the simple textures of brick and concrete that it had been obscuring. It won't be needed, this time. I replace her fallen body with one still upright. I push her forward, place her feet upon the concrete and lift them again, taking care that her shadow follows her exactly as it should. The soup runs out at last, but I don't let that trouble me. I'm so close to finishing now, a few days away at the most. Max still gets fed, we both get our exercise, and that is sufficient. Sometimes I sleep, but only when it becomes impossible not to. Guide her past this next pedestrian, ensure that her left foot lands and flexes properly upon this spot where one slab of concrete joins imperfectly with the next. At some point, when hunger begins to threaten my concentration, impede my focus, I scoop a few pellets of dog food from the bag in the cupboard and chew them while I work. Max doesn't seem to mind. I've become disconnected from the human clock, from the cycles of the Earth. Some of our walks are lit by the sun and some are lit by streetlights. Sometimes the sidewalks are crowded, and sometimes no one but us moves along them at all. These differences mean little to me. Behind my eyes I'm seeing only grayscale, pixels, a possible adjustment here, a bit of shading that might be added there. Details. Everything depends on the details.

One day, satisfied with the frame I'm working on, I try to advance to the next one and find that there is none. Look up, blinking. I've reached the end, it seems. Press save. Always press save.

I repair myself, a little. Take a shower, shave the beard I've been growing for who knows how many weeks, put on slightly cleaner clothes. The shirt I pick off the pile in the bedroom tugs at my memory. Was I wearing it that day, that evening when the knock came at the door, the detectives in the hallway with their carefully sympathetic expressions? Fitting, I suppose, if I had been. Return to the laptop. Press power. Open Reality Plus, and take it in: My work laid before me from end to end now, this sequence of better events needing only a last command to begin unfolding.

I move to press the play button, then hesitate. The camera's footage is best understood at smaller scales, as if viewed from a greater distance. Once I watched it standing halfway across the room from the screen of my laptop and was startled by its apparent clarity.

Rise from the chair again, go to the little closet beside the kitchen. Retrieve a yellow-handled broom, one of the few items in the apartment that Doris passed over. Max follows me, peeks inside the closet. Let him sniff the broom handle for a moment, satisfy his curiosity. Make everything ready on the laptop, set up the video for playback. Choose a viewing position several feet from the screen, making sure that the chair's back won't obscure my line of vision. Max lies down someplace behind me; I wait until he's settled, quiet. Look at this first frame now, its clarity: as real as low-res black-and-white can be. Viewed from the proper distance, perhaps, more real than life itself.

I take a breath, and reach out with the broom handle.

Press play.

The afternoon sunlight shines on the street beyond the convenience-store window. The clerk reads his book behind the counter. The guitarist plays. The low-slung black car drives into view and flashes past, but only once, and then it travels elsewhere, out of view.

Wait, now, silent, until her figure enters the frame.

For twenty-three seconds, I watch Angela walk from left to right. I watch her step around the guitarist, watch her pass by the candle shop doorway without slowing or turning, watch as she takes a sixth step and a seventh and an eighth. She looks real enough, alive enough: one more sidewalk figure among many, no white oval appearing around her to set her apart or strike her down. The other pedestrians follow their own paths, uninterrupted. Nothing to make them change course, no reason for any of them to turn their heads. What this camera captures all day, every day: footage never viewed, never posted, never remarked upon by anyone. Watch Angela leave the candle shop doorway farther and farther behind her, step by perfectly-rendered step. So close, so very close. Don't blink now, don't look away. Watch until you see her pass beyond the rightmost limit of the camera's view and keep on walking, keep on walking, keep on walking.

Freeze on a last frame very much like the first: the guitarist playing, the clerk reading, Angela safely out of view. Something flickers, within the image or outside of it, and the screen goes black.

Drop the broom, rush back to my chair by reflex, lean forward and assess. This latest crash has not only shut down Reality Plus, but it's taken my whole laptop down with it. A flutter of panic as I wonder what's been lost, what's been erased. Max, arriving at the chair a second or two behind me, lets out the smallest of sounds through his nostrils, rests his chin against my knee. No time for him now, though. Reach for the side of the laptop, press power—

No.

Press nothing. Lean back.

I've done all I can for you.

My task is finished, whatever its worth or its purpose may have been. Leave the laptop turned off for now; just sit here and learn what this next moment feels like, what it might prove to be after all this care and toil. I can't remember what day it is, what month it is. Then again, I wasn't sure of that before. Beyond the drawn blinds, the glow outside the window says it's afternoon, sunny. I recall this slanting light, exactly like this, its angle changing over the hours as I sat here in this chair, listening for Angela's key to turn in the door behind me, wondering what could be keeping her. Perhaps I'm wondering that even now? This moment unresolved, so delicate. That which feels true and whole so easily broken, I know. Therefore, make no movements, risk no echoes which might betray the presence of an empty, unfurnished room at my back, might hint at a space or a life devoid of her. Let uncertainty nurture something which might, if viewed from the proper distance, resemble hope.

Are Angela's box springs and mattress lying bare upon the floor in the next room, or are they nestled within her grandmother's bedframe, encased in the pale-blue sheets and the blanket as she left them, beside her nightstand with its drawer full of little totems whose meanings I might, one day, get to learn? Better not to turn and look, just yet. Better not to move my eyes, or leave this chair at all.

So quiet here today, without her. I lay my hand on Max's head and wait to see if she is coming home.

Ж

Made in the USA
Lexington, KY
23 November 2018